Captain Cook's Christmas Pudding

Iris Van Rynbach

BOYDS MILLS PRESS

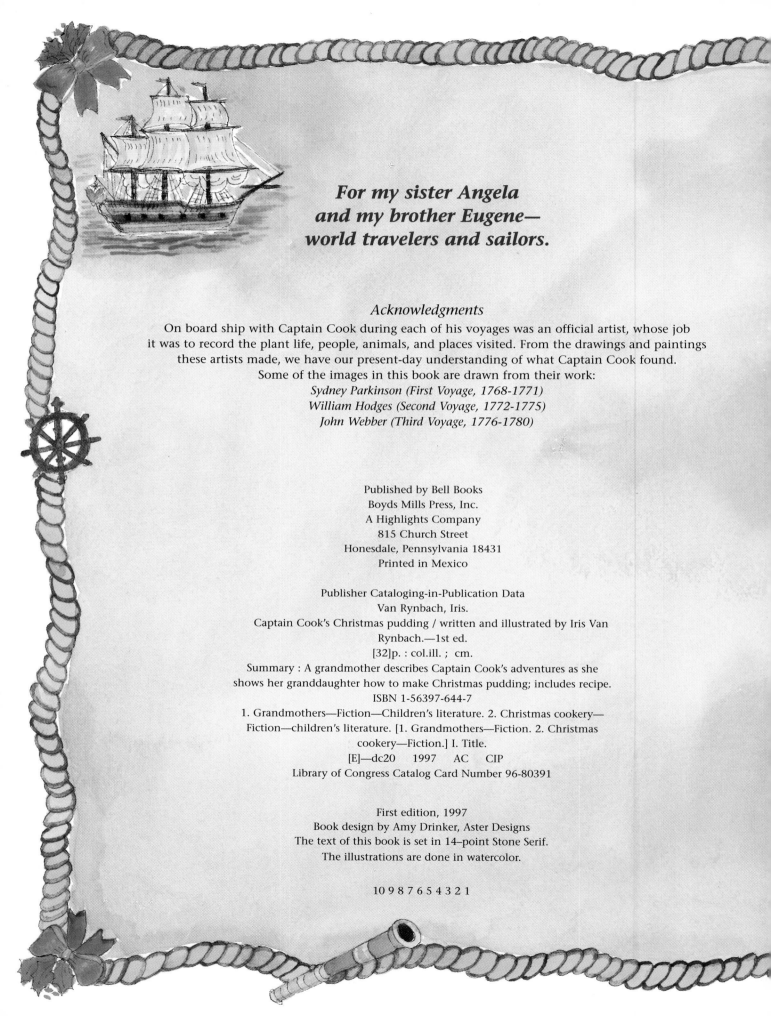

*For my sister Angela
and my brother Eugene—
world travelers and sailors.*

Acknowledgments

On board ship with Captain Cook during each of his voyages was an official artist, whose job
it was to record the plant life, people, animals, and places visited. From the drawings and paintings
these artists made, we have our present-day understanding of what Captain Cook found.
Some of the images in this book are drawn from their work:

Sydney Parkinson (First Voyage, 1768-1771)
William Hodges (Second Voyage, 1772-1775)
John Webber (Third Voyage, 1776-1780)

Published by Bell Books
Boyds Mills Press, Inc.
A Highlights Company
815 Church Street
Honesdale, Pennsylvania 18431
Printed in Mexico

Publisher Cataloging-in-Publication Data
Van Rynbach, Iris.
Captain Cook's Christmas pudding / written and illustrated by Iris Van
Rynbach.—1st ed.
[32]p. : col.ill. ; cm.
Summary : A grandmother describes Captain Cook's adventures as she
shows her granddaughter how to make Christmas pudding; includes recipe.
ISBN 1-56397-644-7
1. Grandmothers—Fiction—Children's literature. 2. Christmas cookery—
Fiction—children's literature. [1. Grandmothers—Fiction. 2. Christmas
cookery—Fiction.] I. Title.
[E]—dc20   1997   AC   CIP
Library of Congress Catalog Card Number 96-80391

First edition, 1997
Book design by Amy Drinker, Aster Designs
The text of this book is set in 14–point Stone Serif.
The illustrations are done in watercolor.

10 9 8 7 6 5 4 3 2 1

Author's Note

Captain James Cook was born in 1728 in a small village in Yorkshire, England. At the age of seventeen he left home to work in the seaport town of Staithes. Within a year, he signed on as an apprentice for a coal-shipping firm—beginning a life at sea that would last the next thirty-three years. Between voyages, Cook spent many hours studying navigation, astronomy, and mathematics. After nearly ten years in the coal trade, he was offered command of his own ship. Instead he chose to join the Navy as an able seaman; he was twenty-seven years old.

Cook's rank rose rapidly, and when it was time to find a captain for an important scientific expedition to the South Pacific, he was chosen above all others in the Royal Navy. This was the first of three epic voyages led by Captain Cook—exploring and charting islands, searching for a southern continent, and looking for a passage between the Atlantic and Pacific Oceans.

Captain James Cook is believed by many to be the greatest navigator, explorer, mapmaker, and sea captain that ever lived. He was killed during his third voyage, in 1779, in a dispute with the Hawaiians.

Captain Cook's three epic voyages took him all over the world. This map shows the places he visited that are mentioned in the book. He sailed on the *Endeavour* (1768-1771) and the *Resolution* (1772-1775 and 1776-1779). For the second and third voyages, he traveled with a second ship—first the *Adventure* and then the *Discovery*.

ASIA

Bering Strait

Hawaiian Islands

Pacific Ocean

Indian Ocean

AUSTRALIA

Great Barrier Reef

Tahiti

Botany Bay

New Zealand

Queen Charlotte Sound

ANTARCTICA

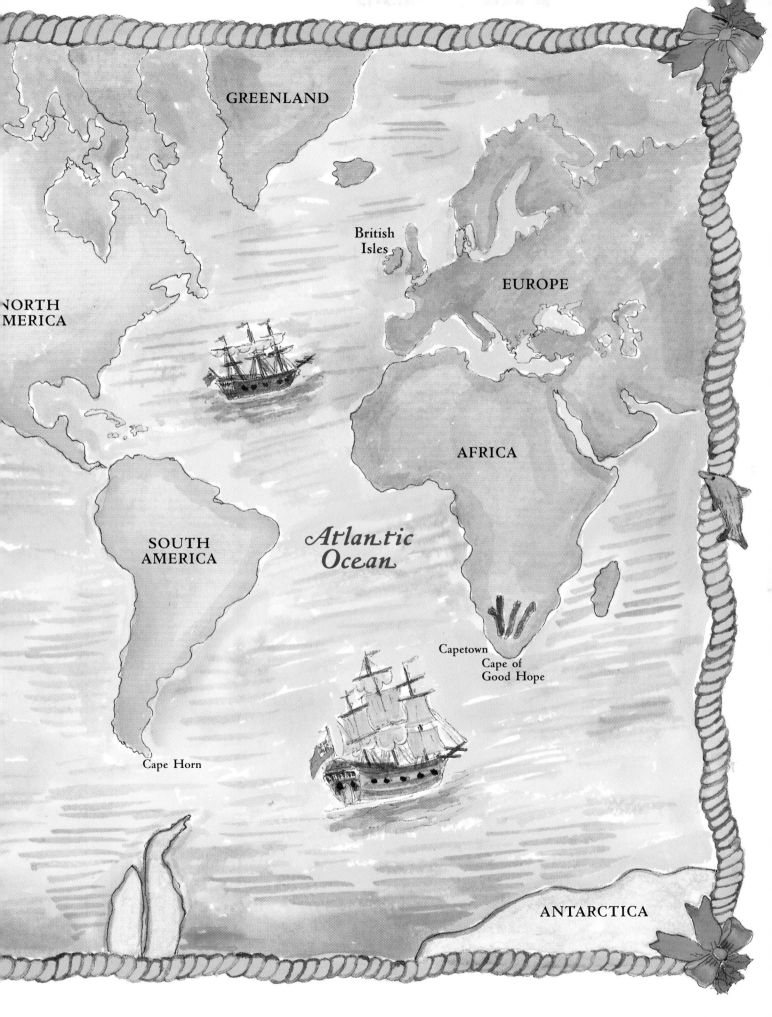

It was Sarah's favorite time of year. Sarah and Granny were making Christmas Pudding.

"This recipe has been in our family a very long time," said Granny. "It was named for Captain James Cook, a famous sea captain and explorer from England. He sailed around the world two times. This recipe uses many ingredients he might have found during his voyages."

Granny carefully opened a large red-and-gold leather book with the words *Ma Cuisine* on the cover. Between the pages were lots of cream-colored slips of paper. Granny turned to the recipe for Captain Cook's Christmas Pudding.

"Here we are," she said.

Sarah leaned over to look. The kitchen was warm and cozy and smelled like evergreen. There was a crackling fire in the fireplace. Granny had decorated with ribbon and pointsettias .

"What kinds of ingredients do we need?" asked Sarah.

"Let's see," said Granny, reading:

one cup raisins...

"Where would the raisins have come from?" Sarah wondered out loud.

"On his first voyage, Captain Cook explored the east coast of Australia, where he might have found grapes—and raisins are dried grapes. A famous botanist on board the ship was collecting new plants to bring home to England. He found so many that they named the place Botany Bay."

"When they were leaving Australia, Captain Cook's boat, the *Endeavour*, struck a huge bank of coral. There was a tremendous hole in the boat, and it was sinking. The men began to throw guns and cannons and tools and firewood overboard to save the ship. Finally the changing tide allowed them to float free."

"Could they fix the ship?" asked Sarah, nibbling a few raisins.

"Yes, but it was six weeks before they were able to sail again. Then they began their long journey back to England, which would take almost a year."

"Where else did they stop?" Sarah was curious to know.

"Let's look back at our ingredients and see," suggested Granny, as she opened the cupboards and began handing Sarah items for the recipe.

Sarah read out loud:

> *1/2 cup dried currants*
>
> *1/2 cup chopped dates*
>
> *1 1/8 cups solid vegetable shortening*
>
> *4 cups fresh bread crumbs*
>
> *1/2 cup flour*
>
> *1/2 cup brown sugar*

Sarah and Granny began to fill measuring cups and pour ingredients into a large bowl.

"What about the sugar, Granny? Where would that have come from?" asked Sarah.

"Sugarcane grows in Africa. On Captain Cook's second voyage he took two ships, the *Resolution* and the *Adventure*. They stopped at Capetown for supplies. The ships carried thousands of pounds of food, gallons of water and wine, and live animals like pigs, chickens, and cows. Captain Cook forced the men to eat onions and cabbage so they wouldn't get scurvy, a disease caused by lack of vitamins. He needed a healthy crew!

On this voyage they were looking for a great southern continent. The boats passed the Cape of Good Hope and sailed as far south as they could go.

Antarctica
Resolution, 1773

"The farther they went, the more ice they found, until it was impossible to continue. Some icebergs were two hundred feet high and two miles wide. To keep warm, the men wore jackets called Fearnoughts made of wool and canvas. The men chipped off large chunks of ice to get fresh water for drinking. They saw whales and penguins and came very close to Antarctica, but never actually reached it. Still, this voyage is considered one of the greatest feats of exploration in history."

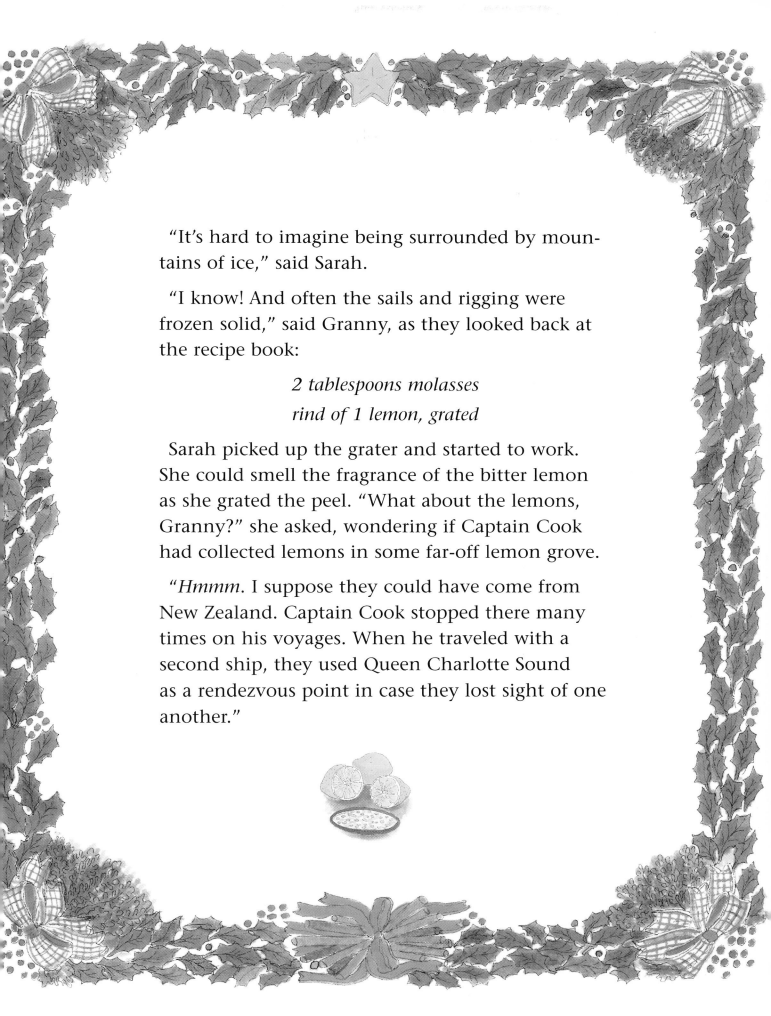

"It's hard to imagine being surrounded by mountains of ice," said Sarah.

"I know! And often the sails and rigging were frozen solid," said Granny, as they looked back at the recipe book:

2 tablespoons molasses
rind of 1 lemon, grated

Sarah picked up the grater and started to work. She could smell the fragrance of the bitter lemon as she grated the peel. "What about the lemons, Granny?" she asked, wondering if Captain Cook had collected lemons in some far-off lemon grove.

"*Hmmm.* I suppose they could have come from New Zealand. Captain Cook stopped there many times on his voyages. When he traveled with a second ship, they used Queen Charlotte Sound as a rendezvous point in case they lost sight of one another."

"In New Zealand, Captain Cook's men again found plants, flowers, birds, and animals they had never seen before. But the people who lived in New Zealand, the Maoris, were suspicious of the strange visitors in huge sailing ships. Fights broke out between the fierce Maori warriors and Captain Cook's men."

"It sounds as if the sailors never knew what to expect when they landed," said Sarah.

"That's true. But the people they met must have been equally surprised when Captain Cook arrived on his ship. It was nearly a hundred feet long!"

Sarah and Granny went back to mixing:

> *1/2 cup candied peel*
>
> *1/4 teaspoon nutmeg*
>
> *1/4 teaspoon ginger*

"What about the spices, Granny? Where did they come from?"

"Nutmeg is a seed that comes from a tropical tree called *Myristica fragrans*. Ginger is the root of a plant that grows in Hawaii. When Captain Cook and his men landed on different islands in the South Pacific, they often traded items they had on board for food or other things they needed."

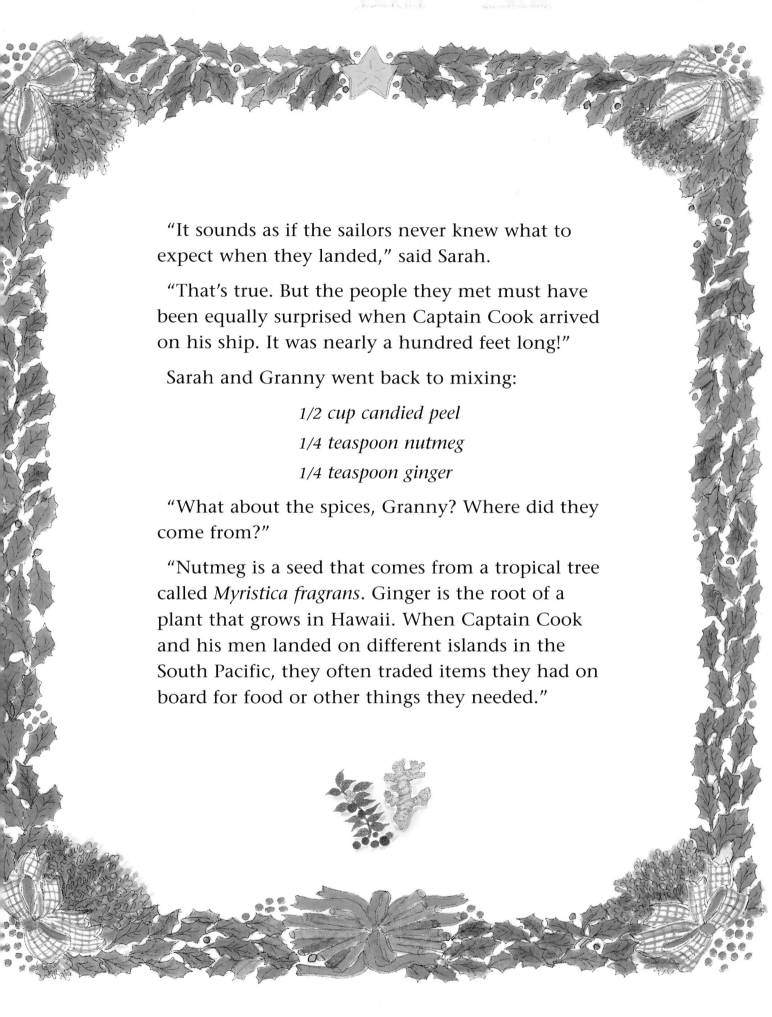

"Captain Cook stopped in Tahiti on all of his voyages. During his first visit there, he brought a group of scientists from England who were hoping to watch the planet Venus pass between the Earth and the sun. Captain Cook and his crew built a special observatory on Tahiti called Fort Venus.

"Tahiti was very beautiful, and the people were welcoming and friendly. There were many kinds of fruits and plants growing—especially bananas, coconuts, and breadfruit."

Hawaiian Islands
Resolution, 1779

"The Hawaiians were also very friendly. Captain Cook visited Hawaii during his third and last voyage. The Hawaiians swam and paddled out to meet him with offerings like pigs, yams, and bananas. They thought Captain Cook was the god of peace and prosperity they had been expecting. At first, he was worshipped by the islanders. But later in the voyage, when Captain Cook returned to repair his ships, a disagreement took place and Captain Cook was killed."

"He must have been very brave, even when he knew his life was in danger," mused Sarah.

"I think you're right," said Granny. "He wrote in his journal that he wanted to go farther than any man had gone before—and he did."

Sarah and Granny added the final ingredients:

> *almond extract, a few drops*
> *3 eggs*
> *1/2 cup cider*
> *pudding charms*

Granny reminded Sarah, "If you whisper your wishes into the bowl when you make Christmas Pudding, they may come true." Sarah closed her eyes and whispered, thinking of dolls and ponies.

Next Granny took out a covered tin and chose three charms—a ship, a Christmas tree, and a heart. These were added to bring luck all through the coming year. The pudding was ready to cook!

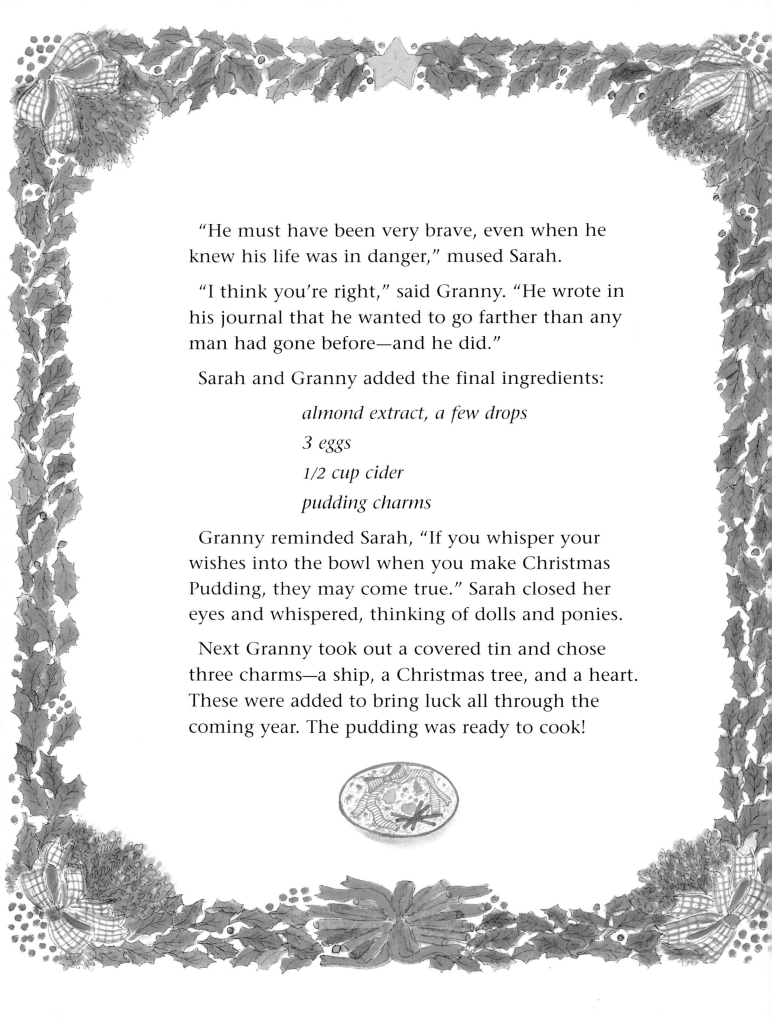

A few days later, Sarah and Granny proudly served their Christmas Pudding to the whole family. It was delicious—full of fruit and topped with a spoonful of creamy hard sauce.

"Look what I found in my pudding, Granny," exclaimed Sarah, "the ship charm!" Sarah felt sure that her Christmas wishes would come true.

Everyone agreed it was the best Christmas Pudding ever—fit for a captain's dinner!

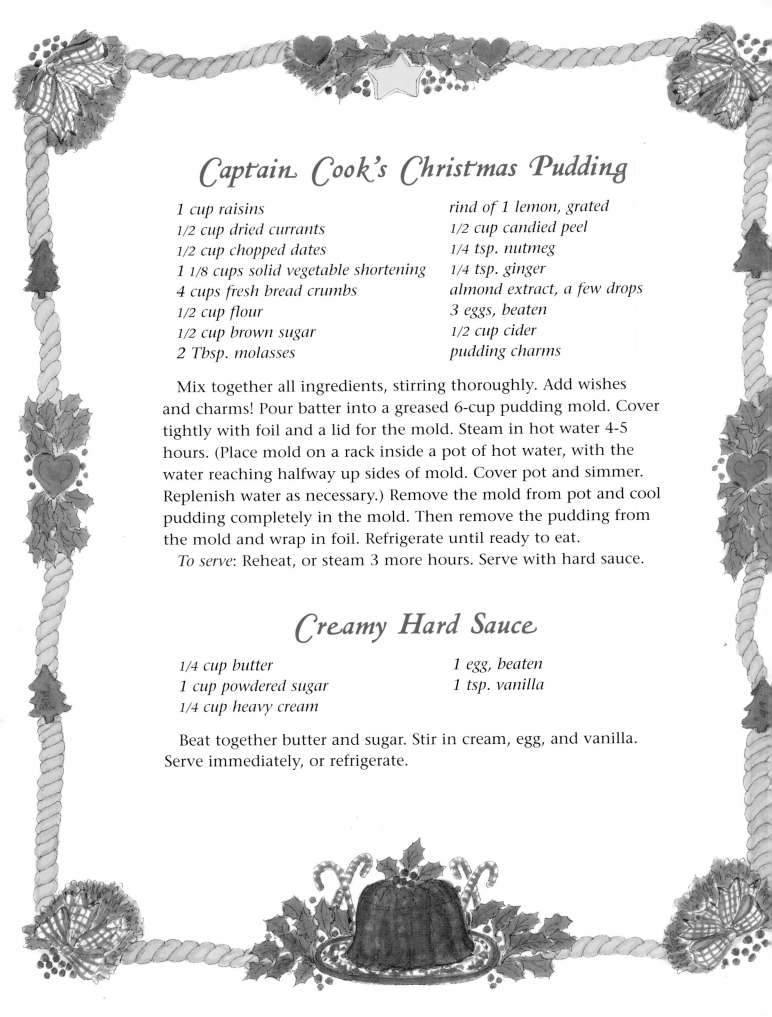

Captain Cook's Christmas Pudding

1 cup raisins
1/2 cup dried currants
1/2 cup chopped dates
1 1/8 cups solid vegetable shortening
4 cups fresh bread crumbs
1/2 cup flour
1/2 cup brown sugar
2 Tbsp. molasses

rind of 1 lemon, grated
1/2 cup candied peel
1/4 tsp. nutmeg
1/4 tsp. ginger
almond extract, a few drops
3 eggs, beaten
1/2 cup cider
pudding charms

Mix together all ingredients, stirring thoroughly. Add wishes and charms! Pour batter into a greased 6-cup pudding mold. Cover tightly with foil and a lid for the mold. Steam in hot water 4-5 hours. (Place mold on a rack inside a pot of hot water, with the water reaching halfway up sides of mold. Cover pot and simmer. Replenish water as necessary.) Remove the mold from pot and cool pudding completely in the mold. Then remove the pudding from the mold and wrap in foil. Refrigerate until ready to eat.

To serve: Reheat, or steam 3 more hours. Serve with hard sauce.

Creamy Hard Sauce

1/4 cup butter
1 cup powdered sugar
1/4 cup heavy cream

1 egg, beaten
1 tsp. vanilla

Beat together butter and sugar. Stir in cream, egg, and vanilla. Serve immediately, or refrigerate.